The Brave little Penguin

A tale from South Africa

Andrea Florens

Illustrated by Claire Norden

Long, long ago, high up on the top of a
table-shaped mountain, there was an egg.
Now an egg in itself is not unusual, but this was no ordinary egg.
In fact, the creatures on the top of this mountain had
never before seen an egg of this sort.
And quite how it got there,
nobody has ever, ever found out.

But there, all those **many** years ago, sat this **unusual** egg on the **top** of that table-shaped mountain.

There it was, all on its own, on a green tuft of grass. Now the egg-laying creatures were curious about this egg, and one by one they came to inspect it.

The blue-headed **lizard** and the stripy **snake** both looked at it rather suspiciously. "Doesn't look like it belongs to anyone in my family," croaked the lizard, and off he scuttled rather hurriedly.

"If it belongs to someone in my family, I wouldn't like to meet this particular cousin in a **dark** and **craggy** nook!" hissed the snake, slithering off as fast as he could.

The smaller birds were most fascinated. Walking around the egg, they considered the shape, the size and the colour. "Never seen an egg quite like it," they whispered. "Well, birds of our size would never manage to lay an egg as big as this!" they all agreed. "It must belong to the eagle!" they decided.

But when the eagle came to inspect the egg that was causing so much fuss on the top of the table-shaped mountain, he shook his head.

"I'm most impressed by the size of this egg, but it certainly does not belong to anyone in my family."
And off he flew.

A few days later, when no-one but a lonesome dassie was sitting on a rock nearby, the egg began to crack. The dassie moved a bit closer, the egg cracked even more. Closer still went the dassie, and with a final loud CRA-ACK, out popped the little head of a penguin.

"Are you my Mommy?" asked the fluffy little bird.
"No... not m-me," stammered the dassie, who was very surprised
to see a bird of this sort.

CRA-ACK!

Climbing out of his shell, the baby penguin peered at the dassie. He then peered down at his own body, and then asked, "Do you know where I could find my family?" The dassie shook his head sadly, "I'm afraid not, you're such an unusual bird, and I've never seen your kind on the top of this mountain.

Perhaps you need to go
down there," he said pointing
beyond the steep slopes to the
land below. And so the brave
little penguin set off to find his
way down the mountain, for there
was nothing else he could do.

Struggling down the rocky face, the penguin came across a baboon who laughed scornfully at the penguin. "Why are you walking you silly bird? You should use your wings and fly like them!" he said while pointing at the birds that swooped past.

Looking at the birds and looking at his
wings, he understood what the baboon
was saying. He began to flap his wings,
faster and faster. He even tried to jump,
leaping off a nearby rock.

But try as he might,
he could not
lift off
the ground.

"You are a curious bird indeed,"
said the baboon scratching his head.
"What are you?"
"I'm afraid I do not know," said
the little penguin sadly.
"I'm looking for my
family right now."
The baboon shook his head,
"I cannot help you.
Best you keep on walking."
And so off went the
penguin again.

After a long while, the little penguin came across two zebras munching on some grass. "Hello!" panted the penguin, who was by this time quite out of breath, and rather hungry. "Do you know where I could find my family?"

"My dear child," said the big zebra, "I haven't a clue!"

"Can't he stay with us Mummy?" said the baby zebra, "We could look after him, and there's plenty of grass to share."

"I'd love to eat some!" said the penguin, and with that he munched on a mouthful of grass.

But, "Fooey!" he said, spitting it out immediately. "Now I know – grass is not for me. I definitely belong somewhere else!" "I must say," said the mummy zebra, "I've seen webbed feet like those before. They belonged to a seagull who lived on that round piece of land in the middle of the water. Perhaps that's where you ought to go," she said nodding towards a small island not too far from the shore. So, waving goodbye to the friendly zebras, on he trundled in the direction of the sea.

Fooey!

It was a very long time before the penguin reached the ocean.
But when he did, he sniffed the air.
For some reason, the smell of the sea made him happy.

He walked to the edge of the water and splashed his
webbed feet about. He felt so comfortable that he decided to
dive right into the water.

And that's exactly what he did.

Oh how marvellous it felt, the cold water covering
his feathers! Oh how easily he swam.
And when a school of fish swam by, he knew
instinctively that he could eat them, and he ate and ate
until he was no longer hungry.

He swam to the little round island,
and climbing out of the water,
he could see in the distance the
table-shaped mountain
from where he had come.
All around him, waddling and barking
were large furry brown creatures.

"Are you the seagulls?" he asked rather timidly. "No, no, no!"
chuckled one of them, "Those are the pesky, fish-snatching
seagulls up there," he said pointing to
the birds flying above them.
"We are seals," said the seal proudly, before adding,
"Are you lost little penguin?"

"I'm a penguin?" said little penguin looking surprised.
"Of course you are!" said the seal. "And if you hop on my back I'll
take you to your penguin family."
And so off they went, swimming under and over the waves,
penguin feeling as happy as could be.

At last they reached a beautiful white sandy beach, with big round boulders... and there ambling about on the shore, and splashing in the water, were hundreds of penguins just like himself.

The story of his journey all the way from the table-shaped
mountain amazed the other penguins.
What a brave little penguin he was!
But most of all, how happy they were that he'd
found his way home.

Published in South Africa by Art Publishers (Pty) Ltd
Reg. No 1947/027008/07
PO Box 334, Howard Place, Cape Town, 7045, South Africa
Tel: +27 21 532 3020
www.artpublishers.co.za

Second Revised Edition 2015